NEW BOOTS FOR SALVADOR

BY SUSAN GASTON · ILLUSTRATED BY LYDIA SCHWARTZ

THE WARD RITCHIE PRESS · LOS ANGELES

EACH MORNING Salvador was awakened by his Uncle Antonio at 5:30 to feed the horses. Salvador did not mind getting up even though it was dark. He loved the horses at his Uncle Antonio's riding club. He loved to feed them. He loved to brush them. He even loved to clean their stalls. Always Salvador would talk to the horses.

What would he talk about?

He would talk about his new boots.

His new boots would be very high and very black. He would tell the horses, "They will be similar to the boots of my Uncle Antonio."

TO VIRGINIA FRAZER OWENS

Library of Congress Catalog Card Number 72-84097.
ISBN 0378-62659-0
Lithographed in the United States by
Anderson, Ritchie & Simon : The Ward Ritchie Press
Designed by Joseph Simon

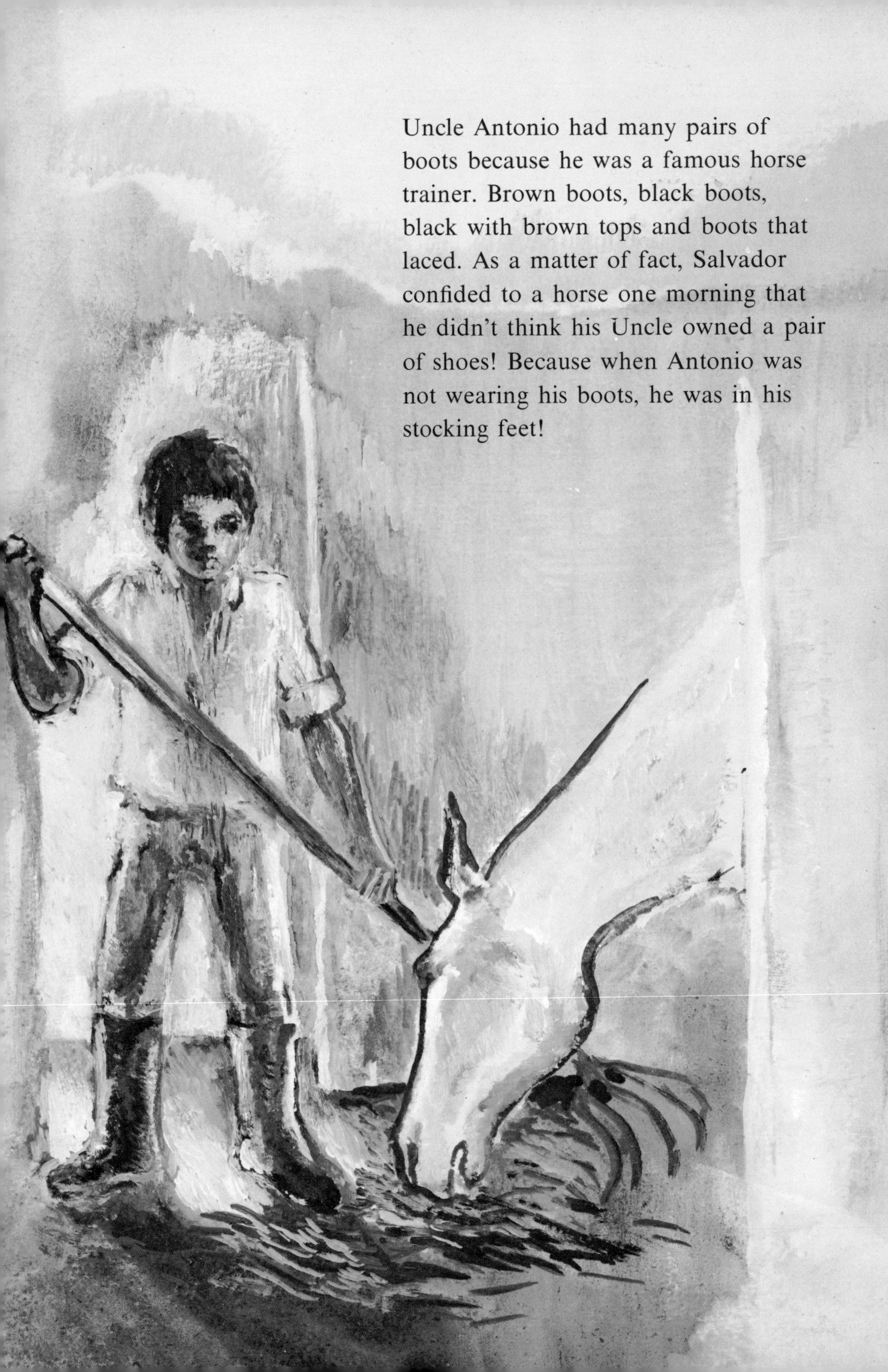

Uncle Antonio had many pairs of boots because he was a famous horse trainer. Brown boots, black boots, black with brown tops and boots that laced. As a matter of fact, Salvador confided to a horse one morning that he didn't think his Uncle owned a pair of shoes! Because when Antonio was not wearing his boots, he was in his stocking feet!

Wednesday was the best day of the week for Salvador. IF it did not rain, and IF his Uncle was not VERY busy, Salvador was given a RIDING LESSON.

For his lesson Salvador rode Pico. Antonio had brought Pico with him from Mexico. Pico was old now but very reliable. Antonio would ride him when he wanted to lead a nervous horse, because nothing frightened Pico.

Almost as much as Salvador longed for his new boots—he longed to ride one of his uncle's special horses, the horses he trained to jump. But for now, Salvador had to be content with Pico.

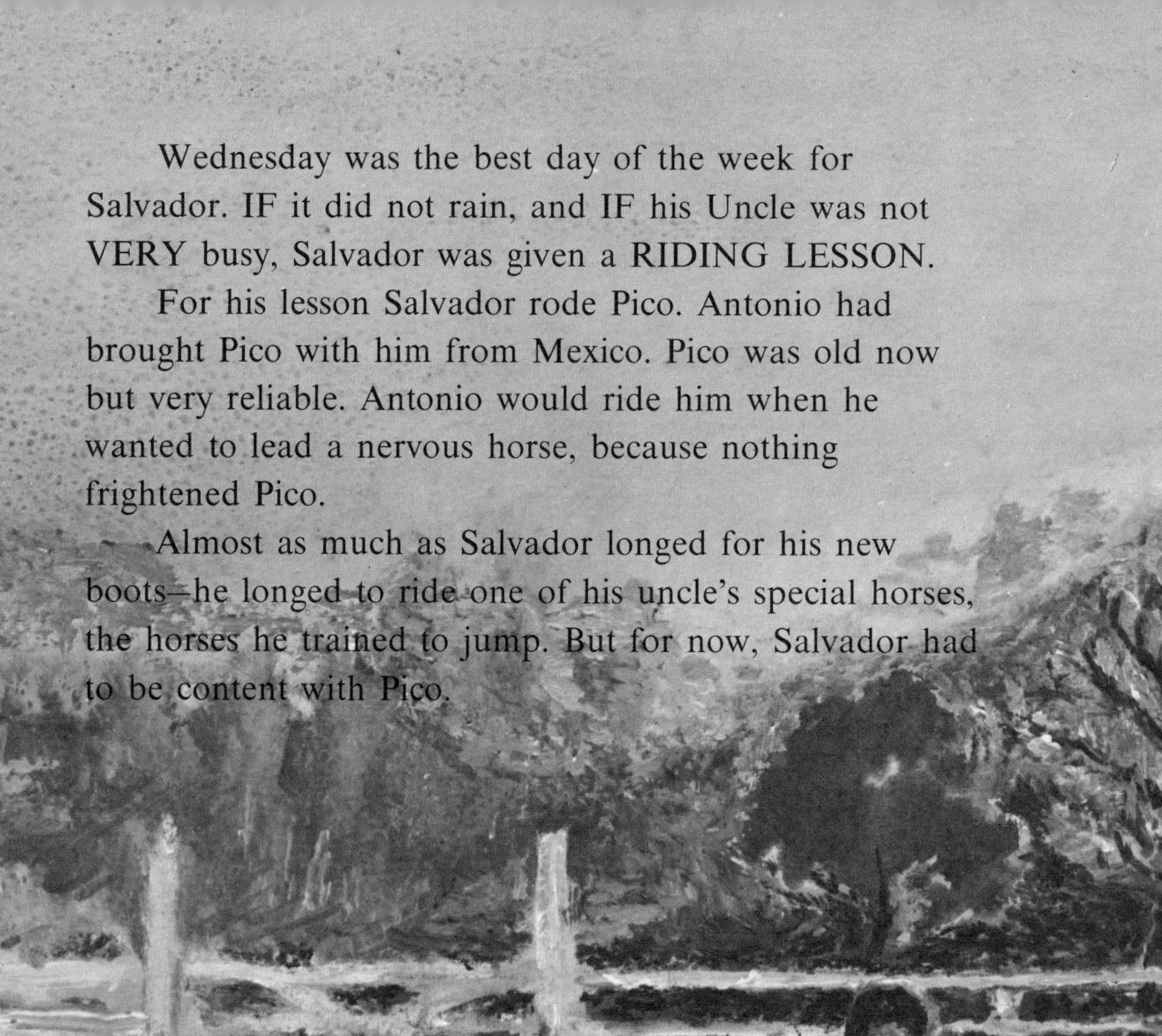

Each Wednesday morning Salvador could be seen cleaning his rubber boots with the hose before he saddled Pico and rode to the Big Ring to wait for his Uncle Antonio. And on the other days, when Salvador would be going from stall to stall filling water buckets, or walking a horse that needed cooling-off before he was put back in his stall, Salvador would watch his uncle ride in the Big Ring. He would watch him working his horse at the walk, at the trot and at the canter. And Salvador watched what his uncle did with his hands, his legs and his heels. What did he do to make the horse go from a walk to a canter so easily? Why did he use one certain bit on one horse and not on another: Salvador had much to learn. When he did not understand he would ask his Uncle Antonio. And one day after his uncle explained the difference between two bits he said, "Salvador, I am proud of you. You ask about what you do not know instead of pretending that you do. One day you will be a fine rider." This made Salvador very happy and even having rubber boots could not change his happy feeling.

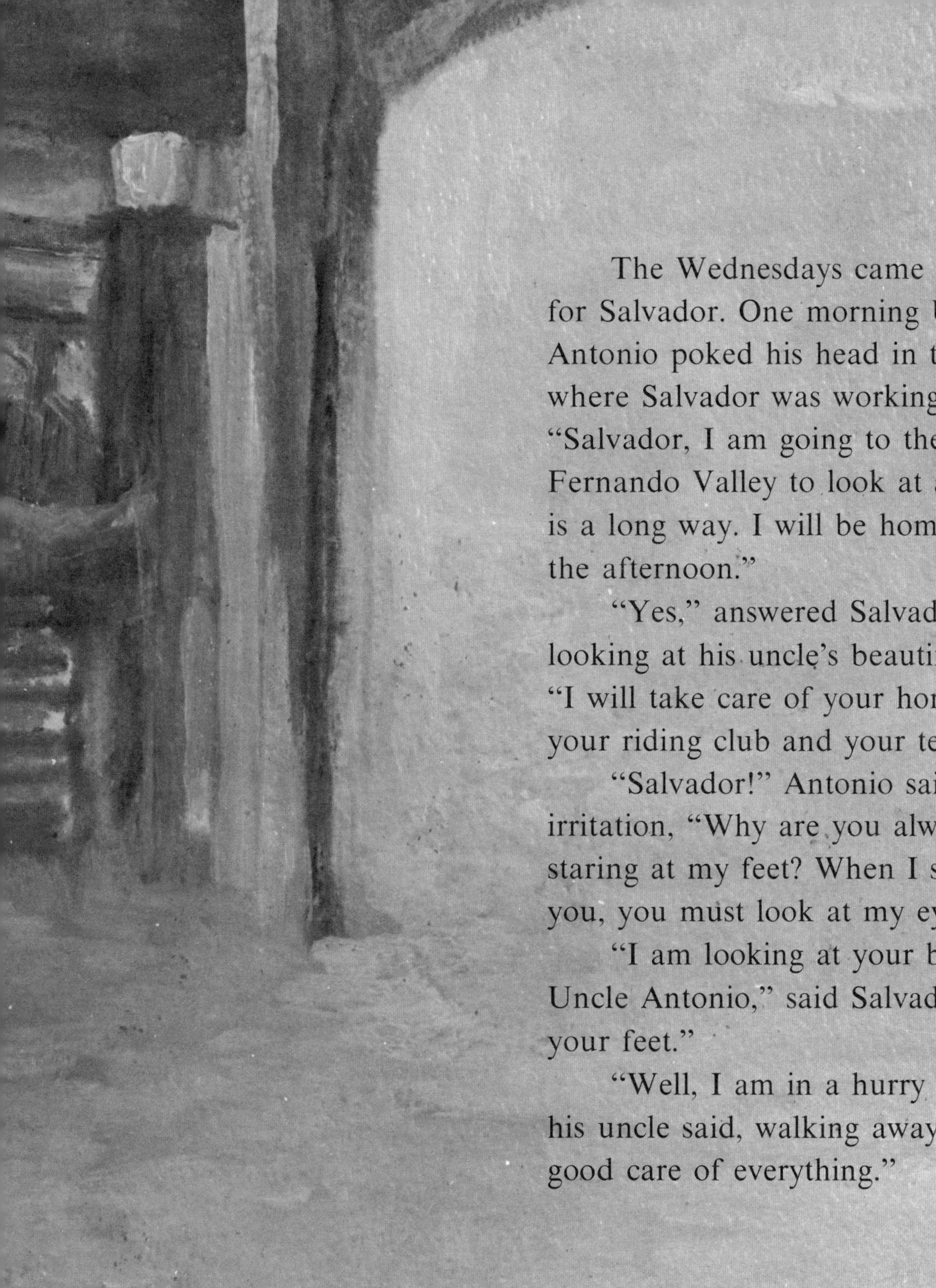

The Wednesdays came and went for Salvador. One morning Uncle Antonio poked his head in the stall where Salvador was working and said, "Salvador, I am going to the San Fernando Valley to look at a horse. It is a long way. I will be home late in the afternoon."

"Yes," answered Salvador, looking at his uncle's beautiful boots. "I will take care of your horses, and your riding club and your telephone."

"Salvador!" Antonio said with irritation, "Why are you always staring at my feet? When I speak to you, you must look at my eyes."

"I am looking at your boots, Uncle Antonio," said Salvador, "not your feet."

"Well, I am in a hurry today," his uncle said, walking away, "so take good care of everything."

"I am in a hurry, too," Salvador complained to the horse whose stall he was cleaning. "I am in a hurry to learn to be a fine rider and to buy some new boots. But I can't learn to be a fine rider cleaning stalls."

And at that exact moment Salvador had THE IDEA. Today while my uncle is gone I will ride a jumper.

"I will ride you, Oliver," said Salvador, patting the big gray horse beside him. "I have always wanted to ride you."

Salvador hurried then to finish cleaning Oliver's stall. He washed his old rubber boots and then carefully saddled and bridled the big horse.

"I will pretend I am my Uncle Antonio," Salvador said to himself in a low voice, "because then I can ride any horse."

But it seemed like a long way that morning from the barn to the Big Ring. At last Oliver and Salvador were inside with the gate closed.

Salvador kept his hands and legs very still on the big horse. What a difference from Pico, he thought. If I make a wrong move, this horse is going to jump out from under me. No, he is *not,* Salvador reminded himself. I am my Uncle Antonio. But I wish I had my new boots.

Salvador squeezed his legs slightly, and Oliver began to trot. Two times around the ring and Salvador began to feel confident.

"Now, am I doing everything right?" he said to himself in a low voice. "Are my hands down, heels down, toes in, back straight, head up? Yes, I think I am perfect. At the trot anyway."

Salvador then brought Oliver back to a walk. I am so happy, he thought. I am at last on a fine horse.

Next Salvador tried the sitting-trot with the big gray horse. This time he held him in a little as he squeezed with his legs, just like he had seen his Uncle Antonio do day after day. Oliver went right into the sitting-trot. And now if my luck stays with me, thought Salvador, we will even be able to canter today. First, I will go into the center of the ring and remember all that my uncle has told me about the canter.

When Salvador had all the signals ready in his mind he turned Oliver back to the edge of the ring. He shortened his reins and turned Oliver's head slightly to the fence. But then something went wrong. Oliver leaped to a canter and then a gallop! Salvador was very frightened.

"I cannot fall off," he said to himself. "I am my Uncle Antonio." His feet in their rubber boots kept trying to find the stirrups.

"You must slow down now, Oliver. Whoa now, please!" cried Salvador, trying to keep his balance as the horse galloped around the ring. "Never keep a steady pull on your horse's mouth," his uncle had told him time after time. "You must check and release." So Salvador pulled the big horse's head in and then released it, over and over again until he slowed down.

When Oliver had quieted down, Salvador walked him slowly around the ring two times before he dismounted to open the gate and walk him back to the barn.

"I must have kicked you, as if you were Pico, Oliver. Is that what it was?" Salvador asked the big horse walking beside him. "I think you are a race horse and not a jumper. And I think I am Salvador the stableboy and not Antonio the horse trainer."

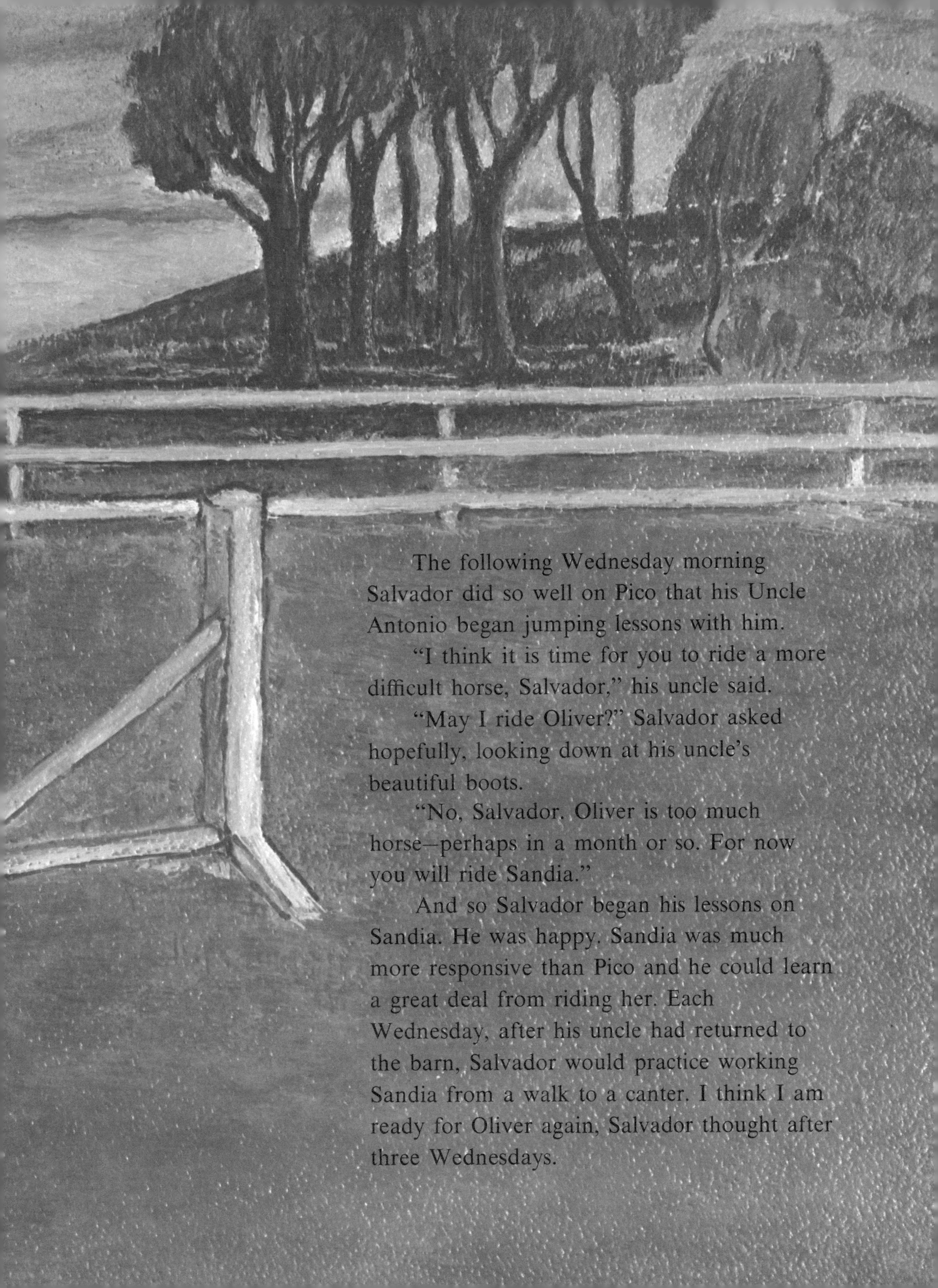

The following Wednesday morning Salvador did so well on Pico that his Uncle Antonio began jumping lessons with him.

"I think it is time for you to ride a more difficult horse, Salvador," his uncle said.

"May I ride Oliver?" Salvador asked hopefully, looking down at his uncle's beautiful boots.

"No, Salvador. Oliver is too much horse—perhaps in a month or so. For now you will ride Sandia."

And so Salvador began his lessons on Sandia. He was happy. Sandia was much more responsive than Pico and he could learn a great deal from riding her. Each Wednesday, after his uncle had returned to the barn, Salvador would practice working Sandia from a walk to a canter. I think I am ready for Oliver again, Salvador thought after three Wednesdays.

Two days later his Uncle Antonio went to town to have some saddles and bridles repaired.

"Salvador, would you like to come to town with me? I will lock up the riding club for a short time."

"Oh, thank you, Uncle Antonio," Salvador answered, "but I think I will stay with the horses today." His uncle could not understand why, but he was in a hurry so he left Salvador with the horses and drove into town with his load of bridles and saddles.

It took Salvador only a few minutes to have Oliver ready to ride.

"My Uncle Antonio will be back soon, Oliver," he said to the big horse, "so today we will have a quick lesson." After ten minutes of trotting and becoming familiar with Oliver, Salvador was ready to try the canter again. This time he had no problems and went round and round the ring on the big gray. Salvador was very happy.

During the next few days, Salvador went about his work, thinking of his riding, and talking to the horses about the new boots he wished for. In fact, Salvador was so busy thinking about himself that he was not aware of his uncle's unhappiness.

Early one morning, Salvador watched his uncle training a horse in the Big Ring. I must polish his boots for him, thought Salvador. My uncle has stopped smiling and hurrying, and he has even stopped polishing his beautiful boots.

"Uncle Antonio, why are you sad?" Salvador asked. Antonio walked his horse over to where Salvador was standing and dismounted.

"I have many problems with my riding club, Salvador. It is very important to me that I sell a horse. It takes time to sell a fine horse, and I have very little time. Next Tuesday a man is arriving to look at Oliver."

"Oliver!" said Salvador unhappily. "He is a fine horse, Uncle Antonio. I am sure the man will buy him."

Now Salvador was worried for his uncle. He talked to the horses. He told them how unimportant his new boots would be if his uncle had to sell the riding club.

The following Monday his uncle went to town to pick up the bridles and saddles that had been repaired. Salvador was left in charge of the riding club. I think I will ride Oliver once more, Salvador thought, although my heart is sad, I must not stop my lessons. And so into the ring they went—the big gray horse and the little boy with the black rubber boots and the sad heart.

"I see my uncle has a jumping course set up, Oliver. They are ready for you tomorrow when the man will come to look at you."

Salvador did not know why he did it. But after cantering around the edge of the ring twice, he turned the big gray horse into the first jump. Oliver jumped it and Salvador lost his balance a little. He pulled the horse in and then continued towards the second jump. This time he stayed right with Oliver and did not lose his balance at all. They went over the whole course, and Salvador had no problems with the big horse.

"Oh, you are such a fine horse," Salvador said, patting Oliver on the neck. "Anyone would want to buy you." Then as soon as he had walked him around to cool off, Salvador put Oliver back in his stall.

The next morning Uncle Antonio said, "today is our big day, Salvador. I want you to brush Oliver and make him very beautiful."

"I have already done it, my uncle," Salvador answered. When the telephone rang, they both thought it was the man calling to say he would be unable to come. But it was the bank calling. Uncle Antonio had to come in today. Now, Uncle Antonio was very worried.

"The man's name is Mr. Harris, Salvador, the man who is coming to look at Oliver," said Antonio. "Tell him I will return before lunch. Show him around the riding club. I will trust you, Salvador, to do your best for me while I am gone." Antonio then left quickly for town and the bank.

Antonio had been gone five minutes before Mr. Harris arrived in a beautiful blue car and a blue horse trailer. Salvador walked over quickly to greet him.

"How do you do, Mr. Harris? I am Salvador. My uncle is at the bank but he will be back before lunch."

"How do you do, Salvador? I am sorry your uncle is at the bank, because I am in a hurry and only have a half hour to see your horse Oliver."

"Everyone is always in a hurry," said Salvador, smiling shyly. "Your boots are very beautiful, Mr. Harris."

"Thank you. I had them made for me in England. Perhaps you could change into your boots and show me Oliver yourself, Salvador."

Salvador looked down at his rubber boots with dismay. Then he said slowly, looking at Mr. Harris, "I have no boots. But I will get Oliver out for you. He is a very fine horse."

Mr. Harris stood at the gate and watched Salvador ride Oliver. After trotting and cantering the big gray, Salvador asked if Mr. Harris wanted to see him jump.

"Yes, please, Salvador," answered Mr. Harris.

Salvador took a deep breath and began to canter in a circle before the first jump. He rode Oliver so well over the jumps that from a distance he could have been his Uncle Antonio.

"You are a very fine rider," Mr. Harris told Salvador as they walked back to the barn together. "And you should have some good boots."

Just then Uncle Antonio drove up. He saw Oliver bridled and saddled. "I hope you have not had to wait too long," he said to Mr. Harris.

"I have not had to wait at all, thank you. I would like to purchase Oliver. He is a fine horse, and your boy Salvador is a fine rider."

Antonio looked at Salvador with amazement. How could he explain to Mr. Harris that Salvador could not ride, when the boy had just ridden Oliver? And also, thought Antonio, jumped the big horse! Uncle Antonio was unable to speak. He could only shake his head at Salvador. Mr. Harris gave Antonio a check for Oliver, loaded the big gray horse into the blue trailer and drove away.

Walking back to the barn, Antonio said to the boy beside him, "I am proud of you, Salvador. You have earned your new boots. Now I know why you have not been going to town with me. But it was wrong to ride Oliver when I was not here, Salvador. It was dangerous for you and the horse. But anyway," his uncle said, beginning to laugh, "now that you will have your new boots you will not be looking at my feet all the time!"

"No," answered Salvador, smiling up at his uncle. "I will not be looking at your feet. I will be looking, Uncle Antonio, at the horse you are riding!"

ABOUT THE AUTHOR

Susan Gaston has been a horsewoman all her life. Born and raised in California, she has been riding since the age of eight. "When my sister and I were children, we divided our time between the Orme Ranch in Arizona and a riding stable in Corona Del Mar, California. Much of the background for my stories comes from those years."

Susan began writing at age fourteen. Her first two poems were published in the yearbook of Saint George's School in Vevey, Switzerland. "From then on my dream was to write as well as ride!"

She lives in Santa Monica, California, with her husband and three children.

ABOUT THE ARTIST

Lydia Schwartz's early training as an artist was at the Art Students' League of New York, where she studied painting with Rico Le Brun, Raphael Soyer, and Jean Charlot.

Most of her paintings have been commissioned, and are in private collections in New York, Chicago and Los Angeles.

Of the present work, Mrs. Schwartz, who lives in Redondo Beach, California, says: "I enjoy using a great variety of techniques and approaches in my work, and found it a real challenge to do these illustrations for *New Boots for Salvador* with the use of only three colors in the paintings."

MAPLE CREST LIBRARY
KOKOMO, INDIANA

ROCHESTER COLLE
MUIRHEAD LIBRARY
WEST AVON
ROCHESTER HILLS MI